DO NOT REMOVE
CARDS FROM POCKET

INDIAN TALES
OF THE DESERT PEOPLE

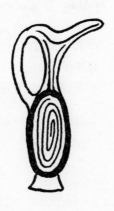

McKay Books Illustrated by William D. Hayes

THE REMARKABLE HISTORY OF TONY BEAVER
—WEST VIRGINIAN
by Mary E. Cober
THE IMPORTANT POCKETS OF PAUL
by Lilian Moore
HUNTER'S HILL
by May Nickerson Wallace

INDIAN
TALES

OF THE DESERT PEOPLE

Written and Illustrated by

WILLIAM D. HAYES

DAVID McKAY COMPANY, Inc.   NEW YORK

VAN REES PRESS · NEW YORK

Typography by Charles M. Todd

TO

Carol, Shirley and Philip

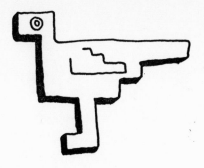

CONTENTS

A Note to the Reader

The people who first told these stories were the Aw-aw-tam, which means "Desert People" or "People of Peace." They lived in the valleys of the Gila River and the Salt River in the desert country of what is now South Central Arizona. They were the ancestors of the Pima Indians who live in that area today and of the Papago Indians who live farther south near the city of Tucson.

When the Spaniards first came into contact with the Pimas in 1687, they found these Indians living in quiet farming villages in the valleys of the Gila and the Salt rivers. It was in the two valleys and in the mountains rising above them that most of the events in these stories took place.

A Note to the Reader

When I was seven my family moved from Texas to this part of Arizona. Our new home was the little town of Tempe, on the south bank of the river in the heart of Salt River Valley.

At the edge of town was a rocky hill—the "Butte," as it was known locally. Beyond the Butte and the river, across the broad valley, were the blue McDowell Mountains and Red Rock (the Salt River Mountain of the stories in this book).

There were mountains in every direction, and I was fascinated by them all. I loved to watch them in the clear light of early morning, in the red glow of evening, in the startlingly brilliant moonlight, and even in the middle of the day when they lay like shapeless piles of ashes in the hot sun.

But there was one that seemed to command all the rest and to brood over the whole valley—the majestic and mysterious Superstition Mountain, thirty miles to the east. Gah-koat-kee—Crooked Mountain—was the name by which it was known to the Desert People, and by which it is referred to in the stories.

We had been in Arizona only a short time when I began to hear fragments of weird tales. Not only were the mountains beautiful; there were stories in them—Indian stories.

There was a flood long ago, one story said. The people

climbed higher and higher on this mountain called Crooked Mountain, but could not escape the rising waters. And it is said that some of the older Indians will not go into these mountains today because they believe evil spirits roam the lonely canyons.

In school, several years later, one of my teachers knew some of the old myths and legends, and she knew the meanings of many of the decorative symbols the Indians used in their baskets and pottery. There was for me a thrill of mystery about these Desert People who had lived in the valley centuries before. I listened eagerly to every legend and myth, every bit of information about the Desert People.

But it was not until many years later that I was encouraged to put the stories down in my own words. The David McKay Company expressed interest in a book for children which I might both write and illustrate; their editor of books for young people, Miss Rose Dobbs, suggested a collection of the tales of the Desert People.

After studying a number of versions, I chose twelve stories that I felt would appeal most to the young reader and that I hoped would also appeal to anyone interested in folk literature. I have elaborated on some incidents mentioned only briefly in the originals, and I have omitted others for which I could find no logical motive or in which the symbolism was not clear to me. At places where I felt the interest and mood would be heightened by doing so, I have written into the stories descriptions of the desert and mountains which were not included in the originals. Possibly the first tellers of the stories felt no need to describe details which they may have considered commonplace. For the present-day reader, however, such details may help bring out the indigenous quality of these unusual tales.

I have kept in mind the simplicity, brevity and color which characterize the original stories; the dramatic incidents and imagery which gave them life; the graphic portrayals of human and animal nature.

The character of Ee-ee-toy, who appears in a number of the stories, is at times difficult to define. His nature and powers seem to lie somewhere below those of Earth Magician, creator of the world, and somewhere above those of the local medicine men who were attributed supernatural powers, but on a limited scale. In order to distinguish Ee-ee-toy from the ordinary medicine men, I have referred to him as a great spirit—a term not used in the Pima tales.

Out of the national life of a people—out of their migrations and wars—grow the folk legends by which these events are presented to new generations.

Among the Pima Indians there was one man in each generation—one man who was considered wise and brave—who was entrusted with the traditions and legends of his tribe. The Pimas had no written language. Their legends were committed to the memory of the *Seeneeyawkum*—the keeper of the traditions. They were handed down from generation to generation. Once each year, in a ceremony lasting four nights, the stories were told before the tribe.

Many versions of these stories exist. The Papago versions differ somewhat from the Pima. And even the Pimas often have variations on the same story.

Those who wish to make a more thorough study of the myths and legends will be interested in the beautifully poetic book by J. William Lloyd, *Aw-aw-tam Indian Nights.* Lloyd wrote down English translations of many of the Pima legends near Casa Grande, Arizona in the summer of 1903.

Carefully detailed but less poetically presented versions of the myths are to be found in the 26th Annual Report of the Bureau of American Ethnology.

The story "How Crane Saved Coyote" is based on a Papago Indian story which appeared in the *Journal of American Folklore,* in the issue of July-September, 1909. It was told by Juan Dolores to Henriette Rothschild Kroeber. Permission to adapt the material was kindly granted by the American Folklore Society, Inc.

A number of Spanish words, phrases and proper names have been absorbed into the language of the Southwest.

A Note to the Reader

This leads to occasional inconsistencies in the telling of stories that originated centuries before the Spaniards arrived in the New World. Therefore, the Spanish terms in these stories are translations of a later period and were not of course used by the Indians in the original telling.

For instance, one of the beautiful trees of the desert is the *palo verde*. This is a Spanish term meaning "pale green," which describes the tree's delicate color. The Indians had their own name for it. But today it is known both to the Spanish-speaking and the English-speaking people of the Southwest as "palo verde."

I wish to express sincere thanks for the kind and patient assistance from staff members of the Mesa, Arizona Public Library; Phoenix, Arizona Public Library; and The New York Public Library.

And my deep appreciation to Kathryn Hitte for her able and generous editorial advice.

W. D. H.

INDIAN TALES
OF THE DESERT PEOPLE

Why the World Is the Way It Is

AMONG the old people of the desert there are those who say the world was not always the way it is now. They say the mountains were not always there, the rivers did not always wind through the great valleys, the sky was not always above the earth. They say there was once a world with people far different from the way people are now, and later another world different from that, and then still another.

This is the story they tell of why it is so:

Before Earth Magician created human beings he created Noo-ee the Buzzard. He created Noo-ee from the dark shadow of his eye, and Noo-ee was black

3

like the shadow. Earth Magician said, "You are lord of air and sky. You shall help me create the birds that will fly above the earth, as well as the trees and human beings and everything that will be on the earth."

But Noo-ee was lazy and left most of the work to Earth Magician. Noo-ee found it pleasant to circle about in the sky, moving his wings only when he must. Anyone who has seen Buzzard circling over the desert will tell you that he has not changed. His movements are slow and deliberate. He circles lazily, floating rather than flying, his shadow skimming the earth.

After creating Buzzard, Earth Magician made the sun and the moon. He threw them into the sky, first in the north, then in the west and then in the south. But not until he threw them into the eastern sky did they stay as they should and move around the earth as they do now.

Before Earth Magician created human beings he created the tall mountains and the *palo verde* tree, and the mesquite and the cottonwood. He created the plants whose seeds are scattered over the earth and grow things good to eat.

Now at last Earth Magician made two little dolls

4

from the substance rubbed from his breast. He placed these dolls on the earth. They were human beings—man and woman. These first parents were perfect. There was no sickness and no death, and the people lived in peace. But their numbers increased until there was not enough food for them to eat. So they began to eat each other.

Earth Magician did not like this. He reached high above the earth to the great round bowl of the sky

and pulled it down. The sky fell on the people and destroyed them every one. While the sky was falling Earth Magician grasped a staff and broke a hole in the sky. Through this hole he and Noo-ee escaped.

Earth Magician walked around on top of the fallen sky. He thought about what he should make next. Then he made a new sky and a new earth. Again he made man and woman from the substance rubbed from his breast and set them down on the earth.

At first Earth Magician was satisfied with his new creation. The man and the woman lived long lives and became gray when they were old. But their children turned gray when they were younger. And *their* children became gray when younger still. At last the children's children's children were gray in their cradles.

Earth Magician said, "It is not right that people should become gray in their cradles." He pulled the sky down as before and again it destroyed all the people. And as before, Earth Magician and Noo-ee escaped through a hole in the sky.

Now on top of this second sky Earth Magician made a new sky and another new earth, and he made other new people in it.

Earth Magician was pleased with his new creation.

6

But after a time the people began to smoke. First only the old people smoked; but soon the young people smoked; and finally babies in the cradles wanted to smoke! When Earth Magician saw this he pulled the sky down again, and escaped with Noo-ee as before.

Earth Magician then began to create everything new again. This time he began with the earth. In the beginning the earth sloped toward the west. Great purple and blue mountains rose above the slope of

the earth into the clouds. But there were no true valleys. All the rain that fell ran away to the sea or soaked into the ground. There were no rivers to hold the water.

So Earth Magician told Buzzard to fly among the mountains and over the whole earth. Noo-ee flew over the earth, dipping here and circling there, the tips of his wings cutting into the ground between the mountains. And where the tips of Noo-ee's wings touched the ground they dug deep valleys. Then when the rain came down there were rivers to hold the water.

For the last time Earth Magician rubbed substance from his breast and created man and woman and set them on the new earth. Their children grew and their children's children. And they lived in the great valleys and on the mountains. They drank from the rivers and ate the fruit of the earth. Earth Magician watched over them and he liked the way they lived.

And that is why the world is the way it is.

Why Coyote Is the Color of the Ground

AFTER Earth Magician made the desert and mountains the way they are now and created the people who live in them, he stood at the edge of the sky. He looked at the whole world at once and said: "It is finished—the people live in peace. High above, circles Noo-ee the buzzard, ruler of air and sky. But who is to watch over the people who live on the ground? And who is to watch over the desert at night? I must create one who lives and moves in and of the night. There must be one to watch over the night world."

So Earth Magician brought the sun and the moon together. The moon came down to earth and

9

went to the place called Sun Striking Mountain. There she became the mother of Coyote. But she could not long care for Coyote because her work was in the sky. She must shine over the earth at night. So she hastily trampled down some green bushes, and on the soft leaves she placed the sleeping Coyote. She named him Toe-hahvs, the name of the bushes that cradled him. That is why in the beginning his bushy coat was green like the green of the *toe-hahvs* bush.

And so was created one whose father was the sun and whose mother was the moon—Coyote.

Coyote grew rapidly, as the sun's light bursts from behind the cloud and as the moon appears full round over the mountains. Coyote was the creature of the night. Even today you can sometimes hear him on the desert howling at the moon. But the moon does not come down to him, for her work is in the night sky shining over the earth.

Coyote wandered over the desert and through the great mountain passes, his shadowy form slinking always close to the ground. Sometimes he came to live with the Desert People but more often he roamed the earth.

One day Coyote was slinking over the desert, his

bushy green tail trailing close to the ground. He walked toward a mountain that was blue in the distance and still blue as he came near. Coyote sat at the foot of the mountain and looked up. The great blue rocks and peaks thrust abruptly from the brown desert floor.

Slowly Coyote began to move like a shadow over the huge rocks. It was a long climb. He panted rapidly, his tongue dripping. At last he peered panting and sweating over a high peak toward what he thought must be the other side of the mountain. But there, cradled between the jagged peaks, was a beautiful blue lake, more blue than the blue mountain. No river flowed into the lake and none flowed out. It was cupped in the crater of the mountain as if in a large earthen bowl.

Coyote looked at the lake. The light of his father the sun flecked the shimmering water. A small bird the dull color of the ground darted into the lake, ruffling its feathers and splashing water over its head. As the bird fluttered about it sang a song:

> *There is a blue water,*
> *In the blue mountains.*
> *In the blue water I go,*
> *And I am blue! All blue!*

11

When the song was ended the bird's feathers turned blue. Like the rippling blue water the blue feathers caught the light of the sun. The bird rose from the water, its song filling the air.

Coyote called to the bird:

"How is it that your drab color is gone and that you are now a beautiful blue, more beautiful than anything that flies in the air? I want to be blue, too. I don't want to be green."

The bird fluttered above Coyote. "I went into the water four times," it said. "And each time I went into the water I sang the song you heard me sing."

Coyote stepped cautiously into the icy blue water, shivering as he went, and singing the song the bird had taught him. Four times he splashed into the water. Four times he sang:

> *There is a blue water,*
> *In the blue mountains.*
> *In the blue water I go,*
> *And I am blue! All blue!*

Coyote looked at his bushy coat and tail. They were turning blue—blue as the waters of the blue lake.

Coyote was so happy he ran down the side of the

mountain and over the desert. His blue coat shone
in the sunlight. Along the banks of the Salt River he
ran, so that the river creatures—the fishes, the turtles
and the cranes—could see him.

Through the land of the Desert People he went,
calling as he raced along, "See my blue coat! See my
beautiful blue coat!" He looked from side to side to
see if the people were watching him. He looked back
and was delighted to see that his coat still rippled
in the bright sunlight like the waters of Blue Mountain. He looked back to see if his shadow was also
blue.

As he ran along, a streak of blue over the brown
desert, he did not watch the ground ahead of him.
The stump of a palo verde tree jutted above the sand
but he did not see it. "My coat is blue," he shouted,
looking back at himself. "My coat is blue! My coat
is . . . oomph!" He hurled himself against the palo

verde stump with such force that he fell sprawling and tumbled over and over on the dusty ground.

For some time he lay in the dust. Then he slowly rose and shook himself. He looked to see if his beautiful blue coat and bushy tail were harmed. They

were no longer blue. They were the dull color of the ground.

To this day the bluebird is blue. Mountains are blue in the distance. Lakes are blue. But Coyote's coat is still the dull color of the ground.

The Legend of Crooked Mountain

THE Desert People say that long ago the Gila River valley was not an arid land, but a green paradise. Where cliffs and desert are now, a forest of aspen, birch, pine and fir once thrived. Through this forest, sparkling streams tumbled down to the river, and from the streams men brought an abundance of fish. The needs of the people were few, and forest and valley furnished them with more than sufficient food and clothing.

Corn, maize, and cotton crowded one another in the fertile valley, while in the forest, hollyhocks, anemones and wild roses thrust their blossoms upward to the sun.

17

Birds, small and large, with feathers as brilliant as the sunset streaked through the trees. Deer and elk strutted about, while at their feet scampered the brownish gray ground squirrel. Bright green and orange lizards darted across the forest floor.

Life was pleasant, and the people lived happily in the valley, hunting and fishing and tending their crops. They worshipped what they saw—the majestic mountains, the forest, the river and the desert beyond the valley, the sunlight that glistened on their copper-colored skin. The sun was their life, and to the sun they dedicated many of their festivals and dances.

Always present to remind them that their lives were not to be abandoned to pleasures only were the medicine men, fierce in countenance and stern in guidance. Where many in the tribe found beauty and joy, the medicine men saw only gods and spirits —jealous deities as numerous as the trees of the forest, ever changing in form and favor, as shifting as the desert sands.

The people lived happily for many generations, but there came a time when they grew restless. Their valley was changing. For many days the sky was neither clear nor cloudy, but the color of the ground. The sun, red as distant fire, was ringed about with great circles of amber light. Anxiously the people watched while dark clouds gathered over Crooked Mountain. At night, flashes of lightning coursed through the clouds and silhouetted them against the sky.

At length above the distant thunder rose the rhythmic chants of the medicine men, and the murmuring voices of the frightened people.

"Someone among you has displeased the gods of earth and sky," said Cia-a-hei, the chief medicine man. "Some great disaster will come upon us."

And the people began to suspect one another and to quarrel among themselves.

There came a day when the sky was darker than before, and the mountains seemed suspended in mist above the desert. The people stood in small groups, talking in whispers. What was going to happen to them?

"Cia-a-hei was right," they said. "The gods of earth and sky are surely displeased. Who among us has displeased them? The sky is fearful to look upon, and Crooked Mountain hangs in the clouds. What are the gods going to do? What will happen to us?"

Cia-a-hei strode solemnly into their midst. He was in full ceremonial dress. When they saw the fiercely painted face and the many-colored feathers, the people stood for a moment as motionless as stones. Then they slowly backed away in every direction, until Cia-a-hei was left alone in the center of a huge circle.

He held his head high and chanted:

> *When the bowl of the crescent moon turns over,*
> *Then the rains shall rain down many days,*
> *And earth shall be no more.*

As the wailing voice echoed through the valley, Cia-a-hei turned and pointed toward the mountains. They were dark blue against the clouds. He sang:

Away to Crooked Mountain,
To Crooked Mountain with my people,
With my people I will fly.

For a moment all stood silently. Then they scattered and ran. The men ran to get their weapons, the women to pack the *seeu-haws,* or burden baskets, with fish, game, corn and pumpkin. The young children ran to their mothers, and the older children ran to help with the packing.

When all were ready to begin the long journey out of the valley and across the desert, they stood again in silence. They watched while Cia-a-hei, with solemn gestures, held his magic crystal over his head and stepped into a large earthen vessel. The vessel rose above the valley and carried Cia-a-hei away toward the mountains. He was followed by the burden baskets, which in like manner rose and flew away.

The clouds, that had hung for many days above the mountains, now rolled over the valley, covering the sun and making the day dark. There was a rustle through the forest, for even the animals and birds knew of the danger. Through the half-light the long column of people and animals marched out of the valley and into the desert.

The dark sky swirled low over their heads, but no harm came to them on their journey. At last they

walked wearily up the western slopes of Crooked Mountain. They looked up, and saw Cia-a-hei standing far above them on a red rock. He was pointing upward. Raising their heads higher, they saw the dark clouds part, and there, hanging upside down, was the crescent moon, pale yellow in a blue-green sky.

As they watched, the opening in the clouds closed with a roar of thunder that shook the earth beneath their feet. Released by the thunder, drops of rain spattered onto the ground. Soon the rain came down so hard that the people were forced to climb above the rising water. Huge waves, as dark as malpais stone and covered with white foam, hammered against the mountains, and again the people felt the rocks shake beneath them.

Through the driving storm the people struggled slowly upward to the highest peaks. There they huddled, lashed by wind and rain. Some cried out in terror as the waters rose . . . higher and ever higher. After many days, the mingled voices of the people were as one voice, wailing to their medicine men. "Save us!" the people cried. "Save us from the storm!"

Then into the midst of the frightened people, Cia-a-hei led the medicine men. They tore their hair.

24

They shook their brightly painted rattles and waved their ceremonial feathers through the rain, splashing as they danced.

The wind and rain stopped. All was calm. Where a moment before peals of thunder echoed through the mountains, now voices rose in song, offering thanks for deliverance. The people moved about in a wild and joyous dance, beating out the cadence on tomtoms. But even as they danced, great thunderbolts split the sky, and once more rain began to fall.

Again Cia-a-hei led the medicine men in a dance of appeal to the earth and sky. The rain stopped. But now a clap of thunder louder than before shook the mountain, and the rain poured down again.

Twice more, with frenzied dances, the medicine men stopped the fury of the storm, but twice more it resumed.

Now, in the driving rain, Cia-a-hei held his magic crystal high above his head. In a high wailing voice he called:

> *I stand on Crooked Mountain,*
> *To escape the rising waters,*
> *To escape the rising waters.*

Then he turned to the rest of the people and said,

"Only one thing more I can do. My power is almost exhausted. Even this can give us only a little time, for the end cannot be avoided." Standing on the edge of the precipice, he looked down at the dark water and chanted:

> *Rise, rise, O Crooked Mountain,*
> *From the evil waters, rise.*

Then the immense boulders rose and lifted the people high above the water. But still the rain came down, and soon the waves lashed at the people as before. Three more times the mountain lifted the people above the flood. Yet the rain continued to fall and the waters to rise.

For the last time, Cia-a-hei stepped before his people. Raising his crystal above his head, he chanted:

> *Rise, O mighty waters, rise,*
> *We turn to stone,*
> *We turn to stone.*

—And he dashed the crystal against the side of the mountain. A tongue of flame licked and hissed at the rain, and a roar shook the mountain as the crystal broke in many pieces.

26

But the light from the flame fell not on men, women and children, animals and birds, but on their images in stone. They had become part of the mountain itself.

When you travel through the Gila River valley on a summer afternoon, look over the Superstition mountains to the clouds banked high above. This is Crooked Mountain. In the light of late afternoon, from the western and northern slopes of the mountain, you can see deep canyons and the grotesque beauty of massive rocks. The rocks rise, one upon another, until the highest are fused in the purple distance.

Across the western face of the mountains, when the late afternoon sun touches them, streaks of gold cleave the massive heights. Some of the Desert People say these streaks were etched there by a great flood that once destroyed the world.

The setting sun is a capricious deceiver. Searching shafts of golden light play upon the sculptured peaks. With beckoning fingers they trace imaginary shapes in the towering rocks. "Over there," they seem to say, "are those not men of stone? And those rocks rising like temples above the others, do you not see

27

images of men and animals and birds carved in them? Are these dead stones not mocking us with a life of their own?"

With one last consuming burst of light, the sun embraces the entire mountain range, and the weird images seem to glow from within. Another glance and they are gone; for the sun is gone, and the sun is their life. Already the mountains are gray against the luminous sky.

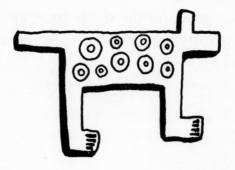

Navahchoo

N O ONE saw his face. He came into the world wearing a mask. He was Navahchoo—the masked one. This is the story of the part he played in the lives of the Desert People.

Early one morning the rain of the rainy night had ended. The clouds over Crooked Mountain had broken to let the light of day through. A rainbow thrust its colors across the sky. The great spirit Ee-ee-toy came down from his home on Salt River Mountain and walked through the mists of the mountain slopes.

After walking over many hills he stopped and looked for a long time at something lying on the

31

ground. It was a large piece of driftwood with four branches, like arms and legs.

Ee-ee-toy picked up the wood and turned it over in his hands. He wondered how he could make it into a human being. While he stood looking at it, the sun rose over Crooked Mountain and shone its rays across the valley. The sun breathed on the driftwood. The driftwood moved and became a human being. But Ee-ee-toy could not see his face, for it was covered with a mask.

On the mask in bold strokes was painted the light of the beautiful daybreak. Against this were painted the bold shadows of the night darkness. And over Navahchoo's shoulders hung a mantle of the gray fog of early morning.

And so it was that Navahchoo, the masked one, came into the world.

Navahchoo reached into the sky with his right arm and grasped the rainbow. It became a hunting bow in his hand. Again he reached into the sky—higher this time—into the Milky Way, and caught a handful of stars. They became a quiver of arrows in his hand.

Navahchoo said to Ee-ee-toy, "Often the Desert People have wandered, searching for the good places of the earth." Then Navahchoo faced the western

32

horizon, and in turn he looked toward the north, the south and the east.

"I am Navahchoo the hunter," he said to Ee-ee-toy, "and I am Navahchoo the farmer. I will search in all directions for the best places to hunt wild creatures and for the best places to grow the things that grow in the ground. And in these places the Desert People will live and be happy."

Then Navahchoo started walking—first toward the west, into the black that swallows the sun. His stride was powerful. Then he walked toward the yellow desert of the north, then toward the east into the light of the rising sun, and last, toward the blue sea of the south.

All day and throughout the long night Navahchoo walked, until the light of morning sparkled on the peaks of Twisted Neck Mountain. There Navahchoo stopped. He was hungry. Out of the ground he made corn and pumpkins grow. He built a fire and roasted them and ate them.

Then he walked on until he saw the white waves of the blue sea of the south beating against the sand. At the shore he turned east. Soon he saw a great pile of driftwood over which flowers of many colors rambled in wild profusion. Now Navahchoo loved all

33

growing things, and he reached toward the flowers and driftwood and passed his hands over them, letting their power go into him. Then he held the power of the mighty waters which had washed up the driftwood. And he had the power of the beautiful flowers, which is the power to make things grow.

Navahchoo made his home by the sea. He hunted with his mighty bow of the rainbow and his arrows of the Milky Way. In the early morning and at evening he liked to walk among the growing things that grew in the ground. These were the plants that offered him the good things of the earth—the fruit that was sweet to taste, the seeds that gave of their strength, the scented flowers that gathered their colors from the rainbow.

Navahchoo's arrows never missed their mark, for they went as straight as the light of the Milky Way. Neither did they diminish in number, for their numbers were as the stars.

One day when Navahchoo was hunting deer near the sea, he felt the earth shake beneath his feet. He walked on a little farther and felt it shake more. Now it was a rhythmic shaking that made his feet want to move in time to its cadence. A little farther on the mesquite and palo verde trees and the greasewood swayed in rhythm to the shaking earth. Navahchoo walked on. Now he could hear the beat of drums and the chant of singing voices.

Soon he came to a place in a circle of cottonwood trees where many people sat, swaying their shoulders and moving their heads from side to side. In the center of the circle was a row of dancers wearing gourd masks pierced with little holes. A low rhythm beat upon the air and flowed into everything about. The trees, the bushes, the ground and the people all moved together.

The dancers stopped. For a moment the air was heavy with sudden silence. Now a faster, louder rhythm began to beat upon the air. The chant of high pitched voices mingled with deep rumblings. Cane rods rubbed a quick cadence on notched sticks.

The faster rhythm brought forth a new group of dancers who jerked and twisted into the middle of the circle. They wore cloth bonnets like the mask of Navahchoo. Over their mouths were gourds pierced for them to sing through. The singers chanted faster. The dancers moved about in a wild fury, swaying, shifting, stamping. The music stopped. The dancers were gone as suddenly as they had appeared.

Soon other dancers took their place with slow,

shuffling steps. Navahchoo's eyes could not look
away from them. He forgot his hunting and he forgot
the beautiful plants by the sea. He saw only the
dancing and heard only the singing.

For three days and nights Navahchoo watched and
listened. But on the fourth day he began to think of
hunting game. He took up his bow and arrows and
walked about over the country with great striding
steps until he found the tracks of a deer. He measured
the distance between the tracks. They were far apart,
and Navahchoo knew that the deer was running fast.

Navahchoo ran to the top of a hill and saw the dust

rising from the desert far ahead. He ran faster. The top of the next hill brought him closer to the fleeing deer. With one arrow he brought the deer down.

Navahchoo hoisted the deer to his shoulders and carried it back to where the dancers still moved in rhythm to the singing. Before Navahchoo could let the deer slide to the ground the singing and dancing stopped. The people fell upon the deer, clawing and eating. They did not leave even the bones or skin for Navahchoo.

When Navahchoo saw this he said to himself, "Even though my arrows do not miss their mark I cannot hunt game for such people as these. When we eat corn and pumpkin and the things that grow in the ground, we eat peacefully. But when I bring back game the people fight over it like buzzards."

One of the singers turned to Navahchoo and said, "We know that you are a great medicine man. You are a great hunter and a great farmer and powerful in every way. You must wonder why we did not join in the hunt and help you bring back the deer. We want you to join us and become a singer and help us to grow our crops. If you will do this you will have plenty of corn and pumpkin and beans to eat, and you will find that such food will satisfy; while, as you have seen, the wild game which you track down lasts but a little time.

"In your mask is power, for it is painted with the beautiful daybreak that brings the sun to growing things. And it is painted with the darkness that lets growing things sleep through the night."

Again the singers sang their songs. The women brought in a feast of roasted corn and pumpkin and set it steaming before Navahchoo.

So Navahchoo stayed with the dancing and singing people. He brought the rain from the sky, for his was the power of mighty waters. He brought the sunlight to the growing things.

At planting time the great hunter spoke to the people and said, "I lay aside my bow and my arrows. I hunt no more. Over this land your seed will spring up and grow and have strong stalks and many flowers and broad leaves. You will remember no more the days of your fathers who wandered hungering over the land. You shall gather the seeds and mix them with the sunbeams. Your people shall eat and be happy and live long lives."

Always at the Feast of Navahchoo he sang the songs of planting time and danced the planting dances. The growing things swayed in the wind. The people danced the dances and sang the songs with Navahchoo.

And Navahchoo lived in that place many years. The people tended the things that grow in the ground. The people increased in numbers and were happy.

How Crane Saved Coyote

IN THE beginning Coyote had been a great hunter. His world was the desert, his time to strike was the night. For Coyote was the son of the moon. He was as the night itself. And he carried himself proudly because of his mother, the moon.

Silently, swiftly Coyote struck. Mountain and desert gave him of their abundance. He accepted greedily. In the time of his great hunting, elk and deer furnished him with both food and sport. His attack was swift, the battle brief. All the great animals of forest, mountain and desert feared him.

But through the years Coyote grew lazy and

afraid. No longer did he stalk the great antlered beasts. His quarry became the little creatures of the desert—the gophers, the small rabbits and the ground squirrels.

One day Coyote was slinking over the western slopes of Crooked Mountain. His eyes darted like yellow wasps as he looked under every greasewood bush and behind every granite rock. Quietly as a shadow he moved, stomach close to the ground, tail following like a snake.

His thoughts were many: *Behind that greasewood bush. No, back of this rock. What is this dark ledge? There, almost hidden, a small burrow. Whose? Nothing here. Back. Around. Over there. Back again. Something moves there. What are you? I have you. You are only a beetle and very small, but I will eat you.*

So occupied was Coyote that he did not see the dark gray cloud that rested on the mountain. He did not listen to the thunder that shook the peaks. He did not see the rain that poured down on the mountain.

He continued to dart about, first on the low slopes, then up a winding sandy *arroyo*. He thought he heard a distant noise, but could not be sure. Soon the noise was a roar.

Coyote looked up from the ground and saw rushing toward him a wall of water tumbling down the steep arroyo.

With a wailing howl of fear Coyote scrambled up through the low-hanging limbs of a mesquite tree. The thorns clawed at him. He clung to a limb, panting and whimpering, his bushy tail dangling almost to the rushing water.

Soon Coyote heard another noise overhead. He looked up and saw a crane flying slowly, her long legs trailing awkwardly. The huge bird settled on a branch in a nearby tree. She sang in a raucous voice:

> *The water goes down,*
> *The water goes down.*
> *I am not afraid,*
> *I am not afraid.*
> *The water is down.*

With each singing of the word "down" the bird dipped a long leg into the rushing water. "You see," she said to Coyote, "the water is shallow. There is no reason to be afraid."

Coyote slowly stretched forth a trembling paw and dipped it in the icy water, but drew it back with a cry of terror.

Crane now stepped down from her perch, first one long leg and then the other. She stood there with the water rushing past, making little whirlpools around her stem-like legs. "You can see there is no danger," Crane taunted. "There is no need for you to lie among the thorns of that mesquite tree. You can see that the water has already gone down. The sun shines upon us and all is well. You are not afraid, are you?"

Now Coyote did not want anyone to know he was afraid. Trembling, he slid down from the tree, the

thorns tearing at his bushy coat. With a splash he fell into the rushing water and was swept along like a twig. His mouth and throat filled with water. He barely found breath and strength to cry out.

Crane felt pity for Coyote. With long plodding steps she walked toward him as he lashed at the foaming water with his feet and tail. She grasped him by the loose skin at the back of his neck and carried him, dripping and coughing, to high ground.

For a time Coyote lay shivering and whimpering. In a faint voice he said, "You have saved my life. I am grateful." He bared his teeth. "Yes, you have saved my life. As we know, I am wiser and stronger than you. But with your long legs you have saved my life, though it was your long legs that led to the trouble in the first place. But you *did* save my life. I shall certainly do something for you some time."

Coyote got up slowly and shook the water from his bushy coat. He walked a few steps on unsteady legs. Then he turned to regard the crane through half closed eyes that were yellow slits in the gathering dusk.

Now his legs felt a little stronger. He took a step toward the crane. His lips drew back slowly to reveal glistening white teeth. Crane ruffled her feathers and lowered her head. Her neck was curved, her long beak held like a spear. She was poised and ready.

Coyote hesitated. The drawn lips relaxed and slid back over the teeth. He turned and walked away.

"Yes," Coyote said in a whisper, "yes, you saved me from the water. But I would not have been in the water if you had not tricked me. We shall certainly meet again. And when we do meet we shall meet in the night when I can see you and you cannot see me."

Scornfully he brushed a little black beetle from his path and trotted on down the slope.

But Coyote never caught Crane, for Crane never went near Coyote again.

The Turquoise Stones

IT WAS early morning in the city of Morning Green Chief. The light was blue-green in the eastern sky. Many of the women wore their brightest, gayest skirts. Their hair was shining black and carefully parted in the middle. This was the day of the knotted rope tournament.

The players lined up, the two teams facing each other. At a signal from Morning Green Chief the rope was thrown high in the air. The sound of shouting and the clashing of clubs was heard far away as each team tried to knock the knotted rope through the goal of the other team.

After long and strenuous playing, the girl who guarded the eastern goal sank to the ground, exhausted. As the other women ran to help her, they saw that she was sinking into the earth and, frightened, none reached forth a hand to help her. The women knew some magic was at work.

Deeper into the ground sank the girl. The women drew back. Finally only the glossy black of the girl's hair remained above ground; then, only its blue-green reflection. The hard ground began to close over her, and from the brilliant reflection in her hair sprang little blades of blue-green grass.

Morning Green Chief stepped forward, his right hand raised. "Let no one touch the grass," he said, "for it has grown not green but blue-green, like the color of the morning sky which gave me my name. Something new is about to happen. Let us wait and see what it shall be. Tomorrow, when the light of early morning glows in the east, we will gather here. Perhaps we will find out why this grass grows neither blue nor green but both blue and green."

Next morning the chief called his people together and took them to the place of the blue-green grass. There, instead of grass, was a large blue-green rock —round like the sky over their land and mountains. In the rock were flecks of light amber, like the first rays of the rising sun.

48

Morning Green Chief turned to his people and said, "As the light of early morning spreads through the sky, so this, the stone of early morning light, will spread among my people. And I, Morning Green Chief, say that this stone shall bring my people good fortune."

The people began to reach out and touch the stone. "She who gave us the stone is gone," said Morning Green Chief. "From the light of her black hair came the beautiful stone. It was like the first cold blue light of the morning star shining in the black that is still night. From beauty came the stone. And beautiful it shall always be. It shall be called turquoise. Come, my people, and take of the turquoise stone."

Then the people crowded around and chipped away pieces of the stone which they carved into many shapes and images. Some were round like the round sky that gave its light. Some were like shapes seen only in the mind, for the Desert People had but to close their eyes to see things that were not seen with the eyes. Then there were earrings, bracelets, amulets and necklaces. Some had open petals like the blossoms that brought the squash. Some were pointed like the peaks on Crooked Mountain and some flat and square like the four directions of the earth.

49

Everywhere people said the stones must bring them good fortune. After a time they saw this was indeed true. Their fields yielded much corn, pumpkin and squash. The people prospered and lived in peace with the other peoples of the desert.

Far to the east there lived a powerful chief of another people. His name was Sun Chief. When he heard of the beautiful blue-green magic stone he called his medicine men to him and he asked them about the stone, and they told him many things.

"It shines with a light that is both blue and green," said one, "like the light of early morning."

"It is spotted with amber like the rays of the sun," said another.

"It is beautiful beyond all stones of the desert,"

they all said. "And most of all it brings good fortune to him who possesses it."

Sun Chief thought about these things many days. At last he said, "Morning Green Chief is powerful. But what if the stone *is* as the light of early morning which gave its name to Morning Green Chief? I am powerful too. I am Sun Chief. My power is the power of the rising sun. And it is said there are streaks of amber light in the stone, like the light of the sun rising over the eastern mountains. Therefore the stone is mine and belongs to my people as surely as it belongs to Morning Green Chief and to his people. The good fortune that is theirs must be mine, too, and the good fortune of my people."

Sun Chief took from his belt a knife of burnished black obsidian, and with the sharp blade opened a

vein in his arm. From the blood he fashioned a large beautiful bird with feathers of deep red. Long flowing tail feathers streamed from the bird, deep red as the blood that flowed from the vein. They shone like the red sunlight on the clouds over the mountains.

With the glittering bird perched on his hand Sun Chief said, "Fly to the city of the turquoise. Remain near the house of Morning Green Chief until you are seen. When they offer you corn do not eat it. Do not eat *any* food you are given. But when you find a piece of the blue-green stone, eat that. Then when they see that you eat only turquoise, it is on turquoise you will be fed."

Next morning, when the rays of the sun were turning from amber to red in the east, Red Bird flew swiftly to the city of Morning Green Chief.

Now the daughter of Morning Green Chief, Light-of-Dawn, saw the great red bird standing near their house. She called her father, saying, "Look! here is a large red bird shivering on the cold ground. Its beauty is like that of no bird of the desert."

Her father said, "Yes, it is indeed a rare bird. Do not touch it, but hold out a long green branch of the

ocotillo plant. If the bird grasps the branch in its beak, lead it here to me."

Quickly Light-of-Dawn found a branch of ocotillo with bright red flowers. She held it out to Red Bird who grasped it in his beak. Light-of-Dawn led the bird into her father's house.

First she offered the bird corn, but he turned his head away. Then she brought melon seed and pumpkin seed and devil claw seed. But the beautiful bird would not eat them.

Then Morning Green Chief said, "Make him some

broth of corn, for this is a rare kind of bird and he eats only rare foods."

So Light-of-Dawn prepared broth of corn and brought it steaming to Red Bird. When she bent over to set down the earthen bowl, the turquoise pendant she wore about her neck dangled in front of the bird. Quickly he sprang forward and grasped the pendant in his strong beak. In a moment he had twisted the stone from its setting and swallowed it.

Then Morning Green Chief said: "This is *indeed* a rare bird, for he eats only the rarest stone of the desert. Bring him all the turquoise stones he wants."

Light-of-Dawn brought Red Bird many turquoises from her treasures. They were carved into beautiful and mysterious shapes. Red Bird took them every one—round ones, square ones and intricately shaped ones. He ate them all greedily.

When he could hold no more, Red Bird went out of the house and walked about in the open place beyond. "We must keep this rare bird penned up," Light-of-Dawn said, "or he will fly away to the land from which he came."

But Morning Green Chief said, "He will not fly away. For he eats only turquoise, and only we have turquoise stones. The bird cannot live any place but

here." So they allowed the bird to wander through
the city.

Next morning Light-of-Dawn and her father saw
that Red Bird was still walking about among the
houses. "You see," said Morning Green Chief, "he
does not want to leave. He will stay with us forever
and bring beauty and good fortune to our people."

At that moment the amber rays of the rising sun
turned to red in the eastern sky. There was a flutter
of wings, a flash of red, and the bird was high over
the city. He circled, then turned toward the east.
Like the light of the sun he flew back to the city of
Sun Chief.

Then Red Bird opened his beak and poured the shining stones at the feet of Sun Chief. Sun Chief gathered them up and gave them to his people, and his people gave them to the other people of the desert. And to everyone who received them, the turquoise stones brought good fortune.

If you travel through the Southwest you will see turquoise stones everywhere you go. You will see that some are green and some are blue and some are blue-green, and if you look closely you will find that some of them are flecked with specks of amber. The Desert People say that this is so because the turquoise is not only the stone of the early morning sky but also of the rising sun.

How Fire Was Brought from Lightning

WHEN the twelfth full moon hung high over Crooked Mountain, Morning Green Chief gathered his medicine men about him. It was a solemn meeting. "I want to know the meaning of Red Bird's visit," he said. "I must know the reason why Red Bird carried away the turquoise stones."

One of the medicine men peered into his magic crystal. After some time he said, "Your great rival, Sun Chief, has done this. He created Red Bird from the blood in his arm. It was Sun Chief who sent Red Bird to steal the turquoise."

When Morning Green Chief heard this he said,

57

"Sun Chief is powerful. I cannot bring back the turquoise. But I am powerful too and I can bring sorrow on the city of Sun Chief. I shall think about this tonight. Tomorrow at dawn I shall act."

Next morning when the light was blue-green in the sky, Morning Green Chief stood outside his house and faced the east. He chanted this song:

> *O cold, blue, shining morning light,*
> *Light of the east that ends the night,*
> *Send cold rain. Rain, rain, rain!*
> *On the people of Sun Chief rain, rain, rain!*

That morning there was no sun in the city of Sun Chief. Though the sun shone over the broad desert, gray clouds covered Sun Chief's people. A rain as cold as the north wind poured down on the grayness that was the city.

The rain fell so hard the water ran into the houses and put out all the fires. There was no fire, no light, no warmth for the people of Sun Chief.

For three days and three nights the rain fell. Throughout the fourth day Sun Chief covered himself with many deer skins and blankets. But they brought no warmth to his body. His teeth chattered. At last, Sun Chief called his medicine men and said:

58

"I am Sun Chief. My strength is the sun. If I cannot have the warmth of the sun, then I must have the warmth of fire. You must find a way to bring us fire."

One of the medicine men said, "There is fire in the skies, for we can see the light chasing itself through the black clouds. Lightning lives in the Hall of the Clouds. We will send Coyote, whose mother is the moon, to bring fire from the clouds." He turned to the door of Sun Chief's house and looked out into the gray evening. He chanted:

> *Toe-hahvs, Coyote!*
> *Child of the night sky,*
> *Son of the Moon,*
> *Bring fire from the lightning,*
> *Bring fire from the sky!*

Out of the gray evening came Toe-hahvs, Coyote, whose father was the sun and whose mother was the moon. He paused at the door of Sun Chief's house. "You have chosen wisely," he said. "I will bring fire from Lightning who lives in the Hall of the Clouds."

Away through the gathering darkness he went, creeping as softly as the night creeps over the desert. Up through the black crags of Crooked Mountain he climbed, moving over the rocks like a shadow.

59

From the topmost peak he stepped through an opening in the sky into the Hall of the Clouds. He walked stealthily through the long hall, his head and tail drooping low. In the distance he heard the roar of fire. The roar grew louder as he moved along.

Presently he came to a great doorway arched like the rainbow. Within he heard the roaring fire. He looked in. There, facing the huge fire, was Way-hoe the Lightning. He sat with his back to Coyote. Suddenly the fire shot like an arrow through the clouds. In an instant it was back again. Coyote held his paws toward the fire to warm them. But he would not go through the doorway.

Coyote wanted to rush in and steal some fire, but he was afraid of Way-hoe the Lightning. "Perhaps Lightning will leave," Coyote said to himself. But Lightning only sat silently facing the fire.

At last Coyote turned away. Back through the Hall of the Clouds he went, down Crooked Mountain, and on to the house of Sun Chief once more. Coyote could not look up at the chief and his medicine men. "I saw the fire," he said, "but it is well guarded by Way-hoe. I could not steal it."

On the fifth day the rain still came down. The medicine man said to Sun Chief, "Coyote is clever and crafty. He moves silently through the night. But Coyote has no courage. This time we will send someone who is courageous. We will send Toe-tai, the Road Runner, for he is not only swift but wise and brave." The medicine man stepped to the door and chanted:

> *Toe-tai, Road Runner!*
> *Swift of foot,*
> *Bright of eye,*
> *Bring back fire,*
> *Or we die.*

There was a whirring noise nearby. Road Runner streaked off through the rain. Up Crooked Mountain he ran, his long tail feathers flashing. Up into the Hall of the Clouds he ran, straight through the great arched doorway.

Like the light of the roaring fire Road Runner ran past Way-hoe. He caught up in his beak a stick burning at one end. In an instant he was beyond the great arch, running back through the Hall of the Clouds.

Way-hoe took up his bow, the Bow of the Lightning. He shot an arrow at Road Runner. The arrow grazed the side of Road Runner's head. Way-hoe shot another arrow. It grazed the other side of Road

Runner's head. That is why the sides of Road Runner's head are still bare.

Road Runner ran so fast the sparks from the fire he carried trailed out behind him in every direction. These sparks fell onto the palo verde, the mesquite, the cottonwood and every other kind of tree. That is why there is fire in all kinds of wood to this day, and the Desert People can get the fire out by rubbing two sticks together.

When Toe-tai reached the house of Sun Chief there was dancing and singing in the city. The rain stopped. The people built a huge fire. Sun Chief and his people were warm again.

Tobacco Woman and Corn Spirit

THERE was a time long ago when the Desert People could not bring rain from the sky. In those years the desert was like a dry burning place. The brown land between the mountains became a land of silence. Here the people forgot how to laugh and sing.

At this time there lived a young woman, the daughter of a powerful medicine man. Through the years she saw many of the other young women marry, but she herself did not marry. In the quiet of the morning and in the evening she walked in the desert and thought her thoughts.

Sometimes she told her thoughts to her father.

65

"I am as barren as the land I walk on," she said. "For as no rain has come to the desert, so no husband has come to me."

One day after she had spoken to her father, she looked down at the ground and said, "I know how we can make the young men care for me. But you must help me. You are a powerful medicine man and I, your daughter, am powerful too. Although no young man has asked for me in marriage, yet I can change into something that every young man will want."

Her father regarded the shy girl for a moment. Then, "What is it you want me to do?" he asked.

"I want you to bury me alive," she replied. "Then

66

I will show you why all the young men will care for me."

So they dug the grave deep, and when she was buried there grew from the mound of fresh earth a little green leaf. While her father watched, the leaf grew larger. Other leaves sprang up. They grew rapidly and soon spread over the ground. "This plant shall be called tobacco," the medicine man said. He pulled off some of the leaves. They turned brown and crisp in his hand. He took the soft white feathers from the underside of an eagle's wing and tied them to a length of hollow cane. In the cane he placed the crumpled leaves of tobacco.

Then the medicine man rolled a coal from the fire and lit the cane pipe. Clouds of white smoke rose up. A cool gentle breeze blew in from Crooked Mountain. It made the soft white feathers of the pipe float like clouds on the air. It caught the tobacco smoke and wafted it up to the clouds of the sky.

The men of the village smelled the new aroma and it made their nostrils quiver. "What is this that floats to us on the east wind?" they asked each other. And they followed their noses to the house of the medicine man. For a while they watched him smoke. Then they made cane pipes of their own, and they all sat in a huge circle and smoked the brown leaves.

The white smoke rose on the east wind and mingled with the white clouds above. The clouds became dark. A bolt of lightning flashed over the desert and split the sky apart. When the sky came together again it sent a great peal of thunder echoing between the mountains.

The people stood and watched the sky. A single drop of rain fell on the medicine man. Then more drops fell and soon a great rainstorm lashed the desert. The people shouted for joy. They joined hands and danced about, splashing in the rain and letting it fall over their faces.

Their shouts mingled with the thunder: "The tobacco plant has brought the rain!" "The woman buried alive has saved us!"

And they planted corn and the corn grew tall and straight. And Corn Spirit, who watched over their crops, rejoiced with them.

When the time came for gathering the corn, Tobacco Woman rose from her grave through the stalk of the green plant. In her father's house she stood quietly by, watching the men. They were seated in a circle, smoking their cane pipes. Tobacco Woman took up her life again and went on living in the village as before. No man asked for her in marriage, but she smiled when she saw how much all the men cared for the brown leaves.

Now Tobacco Woman and Corn Spirit began to spend much time together. "This is good," the Desert People said. "For to be happy, we must have corn, and rain to make it grow. Yes, it is good that Tobacco Woman and Corn Spirit are together. Perhaps they may even marry."

But Tobacco Woman and Corn Spirit began to quarrel over which of them was more important to the village.

"The desert is barren without rain," said Tobacco Woman, "and I bring the rain."

"That is so," Corn Spirit said. "Corn cannot grow without rain. But the people know that long before you lived there was rain in the desert. And the corn grew tall and the people were happy. But now the women laugh at you because you act as one of importance and you are not at all important."

Corn Spirit pointed to one of the houses. "Do you hear the laughter there?" he asked. "And those women walking there—see, they are laughing at you too."

Now the Desert People were a laughing people.

69

Often you could hear their laughter just before mid-day or in the quiet of early evening. Many times Tobacco Woman had laughed with them or heard their laughter from far away and was glad for them.

But now when she heard the people laughing, she thought they were laughing at her. So she ran back to her father's house and sank down on the floor and buried her face in her hands.

Tobacco Woman was no longer happy in the village. She left her father's house and wandered across the desert toward the setting sun. For many days she walked until at last she came to the Colorado River. With powerful strokes she swam across the wide river to the land of the Mohaves, to Cheof-toe-ahk—Tall Mountain. Here she lived.

Many moons grew round and slender again. Tobacco Woman stood on a high cliff looking to the east, toward her people. When the people of Tobacco Woman's village went to pick the tobacco leaves the plant was gone. The days grew long and corn planting time came. But no rain fell and the corn was parched in the ground. None grew and none sprouted.

So the people cried out in anger to Corn Spirit. "When Tobacco Woman lived here," they said, "there was much rain. But you made her leave us and now no clouds come to our skies. Even though the medicine men wave the white cloud-like feathers and lift their voices to the skies, the skies do not answer." So the people sent Corn Spirit away.

Corn Spirit traveled toward the east, singing as he went:

> *To the east I go,*
> *Away from a dry and thirsty land.*
> *To the east I go,*
> *Where there will be rain,*
> *Where there will be rain.*

Corn Spirit took with him his pets, the blackbirds. He scattered kernels of corn as he went so the birds would follow him.

Now Gee-hee-sop—Chief Red Bird, of Tobacco Woman's village—was a powerful medicine man. He looked into his magic crystal and saw that Tobacco Woman was at Tall Mountain. Swiftly he went to her. "Our people need you," he told her. "There is no rain. The people are sad and laugh no more. We have sent Corn Spirit away and we want you to come back to us."

So Tobacco Woman went back to the village with Chief Red Bird. And when the people saw her they were glad. And the tobacco leaves grew again and the men smoked their cane pipes and once more the rain came down.

Far away in the eastern lands Corn Spirit wandered through great valleys and over high mountains. But no rain fell there. So Corn Spirit turned westward again, with his pets, the blackbirds.

After a long journey through the dry land they came to Crooked Mountain. They walked around the mountain to the western slopes. Here they lived for a while where they could look out over the valley to the land of the Desert People.

One morning Corn Spirit saw a woman from his village. She and her younger brother were gathering and roasting white cactus.

At first the woman did not see him. But when she looked into the roasting vessel she saw not cactus but corn and pumpkin mixed together and steaming. She knew that someone had worked magic, and looking up, recognized Corn Spirit.

"How is it with the people of our village?" Corn Spirit asked.

"The people are well," she answered, "but there is not enough to eat."

"And has there been rain?"

"There has been rain."

"Then Tobacco Woman is with you again."

"Yes, she is with us again."

74

"How are your crops?"

"Our crops are few. The corn will not grow when you are not with us."

"Is Tobacco Woman married?"

"No, she is not married."

Corn Spirit was silent. Then he said, "I want you to send your brother to Tobacco Woman's father. Tell him that I want Tobacco Woman to be my wife."

Corn Spirit and the woman waited at Crooked Mountain while the boy went back to the village. Slowly the sun moved toward the western mountains. The shadows were growing long when the boy returned.

"Tobacco Woman's father sent her answer," he said. "Her answer is yes. She will marry you. The people welcome you back. They will build a house for you and Tobacco Woman. They will make it of cane mats instead of bushes, for they want it to be the best."

When the sky gleamed red in the west, Corn Spirit walked toward the village. Hovering over him was a great black cloud that moved along with him as he walked. As he came closer, the cloud grew bigger, and the people who had gathered to welcome him

75

could see that it was a cloud of blackbirds. They knew Corn Spirit was bringing his pets home with him.

And Corn Spirit and Tobacco Woman were married and went to live in the house of cane mats. All through the night a great cloud hovered over the house of Corn Spirit and Tobacco Woman. The cloud sent down not rain—but corn and pumpkins!

When the time came to put the corn in the ground the people sent white clouds of smoke soaring. These mingled with the clouds of the sky and the rain came down. The corn and pumpkins grew and the people were happy.

Ever since that time the Desert People have grown corn and pumpkins. And wherever corn is growing you will always find Corn Spirit's pets, the blackbirds.

Man-Eagle

THERE lived near Salt River Mountain a gambler named Vandai. He was so successful that he won everything of value in Salt River valley.

Sometimes he played the gainscoot, or dice sticks. Sometimes he played the game of the guessing sticks. A stranger with turquoise earrings would ride by on a fine horse. "Which stick do I have in my hand," Vandai would say, "the red or the blue?" If the stranger was foolish enough to stop, he left on foot, for Vandai won his horse and his jewelry, and sometimes even his wives.

No event was too small or too large on which to bet. "That bluebird perched on the mesquite there," he would say, "I think it will fly toward the south." If this challenge attracted a wager, as it usually did, the bird flew toward the south!

"There is not a cloud in the sky today, but I believe there will be rain tomorrow," he would say, smiling and nodding his head. If he tempted someone to wager, the next day dawned bleak and gray.

After Vandai won all the precious possessions of his own people, there came gamblers from far away beyond the mountains. They had heard of this man who could not lose, and each wanted to be the first to beat Vandai. But each in turn lost all he had, and Vandai grew rich.

There was much grumbling among his victims and one day a chief went to see the great spirit Ee-ee-toy in his home on Salt River Mountain. "I have lost all my wives to Vandai," the chief said, "and all my beautiful carved turquoise and my brilliantly colored feather cloaks. Will you give me something to wager against this gambler? This time I feel I can surely beat him."

Ee-ee-toy gave the chief a cloak made of brightly colored hummingbird feathers and said, "I will go with you, for I want to see how this Vandai always wins."

Together they went down the mountain toward the village of Vandai. From a great way off they could see the gambler's house, and around it the bows, arrows, turquoise, feather cloaks, shields and spears. All the hoard of Vandai's wealth glistened in the sunlight.

The game was easily arranged. When Vandai and the chief began to throw the gainscoot, Ee-ee-toy watched carefully. He saw that these were like no other dice sticks, for they had been made by a medicine man whose power was very great.

Ee-ee-toy said to himself, "As powerful as I am, I cannot destroy the power of these magic dice sticks. But although I cannot change *them,* yet I can change Vandai."

Over the desert Ee-ee-toy walked until he came to the village of a powerful medicine man. He said to the medicine man, "You must send your daughter to the tall cottonwood trees by the river. There she must gather many feathers of hawks, buzzards and eagles. She must bring the feathers to me." And the medicine man sent his daughter, and she gathered a bundle of large feathers and brought them to Ee-ee-toy.

He took them and scraped the pith out of the shafts and cleaned every feather. He cut the feathers into small pieces and put them into an earthen pot and said to the girl, "Roast these in this pot. Roast them well over the hottest hot fire."

The girl bent over the pit and placed the pot of feathers on the fire. While the feathers roasted she looked into the pot. The feathers were curled. She saw in the pot the image of an eagle's wing. Then she saw the image of an eagle's talons. The images went away and the feathers looked like roasted corn.

Ee-ee-toy said to her, "Now roast some real corn

80

and mix it well with the feathers. Then grind them all together until they are ground very fine, and mix them with water. When you go to the reservoir for water take with you in your burden basket five *ollas* filled with this *pinole* of feathers and corn."

When the girl was ready to leave, Ee-ee-toy said, "On the way to the reservoir you will pass by a place where Vandai is playing gainscoot with three men. He will follow you to the reservoir and ask you to marry him. You must be polite to him, but do not look directly at him, for, although he is good to look upon, his character is bad. Tell him that he must speak to your parents. Then give him the pinole to drink."

"But Vandai will not see me," said the girl. "When he gambles, he sees only the dice sticks and his winnings."

"He will look up when you pass by," said Ee-ee-toy, "and he will forget the dice sticks. When he sees you he will think only of you and will do as you ask. He will drink the pinole."

So the girl took the ollas filled with the pinole and put them into her seeu-haw, her burden basket. As smoothly as birds flying she walked with the basket on her back, held by a strap over her forehead. When she came to the place where Vandai was gambling with the three men she did not look directly at them. She held her head high and walked on toward the reservoir.

Vandai paused with the dice sticks and said to the men, "I am thirsty. Before we play any more I must have water."

"There is water in the olla under the mesquite tree," said one of the men.

"But I would rather go to the reservoir," Vandai said. "You can be making holes for the game until I get back."

So Vandai followed the girl to the reservoir. He stood quietly for a time watching her. Then, "You are very beautiful," he said. "I want you to be my wife."

The girl remembered what Ee-ee-toy had told her. She did not look up at Vandai. Instead, she looked at his reflection in the water. For a few moments she hesitated. Then she closed her eyes and said, "I want you to drink some of this pinole, and when the sun is setting you may go to my parents and speak to them."

She gave him an olla. He took it and drank from it. Beads of sweat stood out on his forehead. She gave him a second olla. When he drank from it his skin became rough like the skin of a plucked goose.

82

She gave him a third olla. This time when he drank, feathers began to grow all over his body. Then she gave him a fourth olla and long feathers grew from his arms. And when he drank from the fifth olla his nose changed to a beak and his nails to talons.

With the piercing cry of an eagle Vandai flew up and perched on the high bank of the reservoir. He watched the girl through black and yellow eyes that shone like fire.

The girl left her ollas and burden basket and ran back to the village. "Come see the terrible thing that has happened to Vandai," she shouted. "Vandai has changed into an eagle! Vandai the gambler is an eagle!"

When the people saw the man-eagle, some fainted with terror. Others ran to get their bows and arrows.

Bowstrings twanged as many warriors shot their arrows at Vandai. Soon the sky was dark with flying arrows, but Vandai grasped them in his talons and the arrows did not pierce him.

Vandai stretched his wings and began to hop around. At first he rose only a little way above the ground. Then he flew higher and perched on the limb of a mesquite tree. He had already grown so large the tree was crushed. He flew to another tree. That, too, was crushed.

Now Vandai flapped his great wings and rose above the valley. He circled about over the villages, then turned east toward Crooked Mountain.

It took Vandai but a little while to reach the mountain. He came to rest at the foot of a high red bluff. But the rocks rolled from beneath his feet and crashed into the canyon below. Vandai flew higher and perched on the edge of a cliff. The cliff swayed and shook beneath him. But after a time all was still. He clutched the edge with his talons and ruffled his feathers. He clung there looking to the west, out over the valley of the Salt River.

Some of the old Desert People say it was foretold from the beginning that one of the race of men would be changed into an eagle. In olden times parents warned their children:

"Practice virtue or you may be changed into an eagle. For it is said some good-looking bad person

will be so transformed. So it shall be, for so it has been foretold from the beginning."

Some of the Desert People of recent times say the Americans must have known Vandai. "You can see him on the silver dollar," they say, "grasping the arrows in his talons."

Wampum Eater and the Canal

THERE were years of peace in the olden times when the Desert People were increasing in numbers and were moving from place to place. They wandered over vast stretches of barren desert and into dry valleys, always looking for seeds of the mesquite tree and other plants.

Some of the people went south into the Papago country. Some went into the Gila River valley and some into the Salt River valley.

Some of the people settled in a place south of the Salt River where they could hear the water tumbling over the rocks. They could look to the northeast and see Salt River Mountain, and to the east and see

Crooked Mountain. A fringe of dusty cottonwood trees clung to the river's edge. Southward the desert stretched away toward the blue mountains.

Life was not easy in this dry land. The people gathered mesquite beans and pounded them into sweet cakes. The red fruit of the *har-san*—the giant cactus—they made into a jam and sealed in earthen jars. But sometimes the people could find nothing at all to eat and then there were many days without any food.

At such times the people went to their kinsmen across the river and the kinsmen gave generously of their corn, squash and pumpkin. These kinsmen had brought water from the river through a large canal which they dug in the hard ground with their hands and with sharp stones. From the canal they dug small ditches which carried the water to their fields. And that was why their fields were fat with good things to eat. That was why they could share their corn and squash and pumpkin and melons with the people from the dry land south of the river.

There came a time when the people south of the river met together. Their chief spoke to them.

"We must dig a canal," he said. "We must ask the river to smile on us and give us water for our crops.

We must lead the river to our fields, as our kinsmen have led it to theirs."

The men and women dragged the thorny mesquite limbs and the greasewood bushes into the river. They weighted the limbs down with rocks and piled the bushes against them. Then they hacked away the sand and rock and dug a canal south to their fields.

They lifted the rock gate and let the river water flow into the canal. But the water trickled only a short distance and then stopped. It would flow no farther because the canal ran uphill. The rock through which they dug was lime rock and they could dig no deeper.

"We must call on someone stronger than we," they said. And they sent Coyote to the great spirit Ee-ee-toy.

Ee-ee-toy came down from his home on Salt River Mountain. He showed the people how to make sharp stakes of ironwood. The people stood in a row with their pointed stakes in their hands. Ee-ee-toy sang:

> *Through hard lime rock we dig,*
> *Through hard lime rock we dig.*
> *Strike! Ee-yah!*

With their stakes the people struck the rock. The

89

points splintered with a cracking noise heard far away. They struck many times and sang as Ee-ee-toy sang, but they could not dig in the hard rock.

Then Ee-ee-toy said, "I can do no more, but there is an old woman who may be able to help you. Her name is Wampum Eater, and though only a woman she is very wise. Ask her to help you."

Swift runners were sent to the mountain home of Wampum Eater. When they told her that neither the people nor Ee-ee-toy could dig the canal she said, "I will come at once. I will dig the canal for you."

"Our people will wait for you in the village," the chief runner said, and they raced back with the news.

Wampum Eater came as she promised. But no one in the village saw her, for she brought the mountain mists with her. The people saw only fog hovering over the river.

Wampum Eater did not go to the people waiting for her in the village. She went straight to the mouth of the canal, to the place in the rock where the canal began to run up hill. She stopped and took a deep breath. Then she puffed out her cheeks and blew on the hard limestone. Her breath dug into the limestone and threw the rocks out on either side of the canal.

Then she turned to the fog and said:

Hold back the river's water, O fog.
Hold it back for my people!

The fog moved across the river and held to the cottonwood trees. In this way it forced the river back so the cold blue water flowed through the stone headgate into the canal and stretched away to the fields.

Wampum Eater saw that her work was done. She gathered the foggy mountain mist about her and went back to her home.

Early next morning a boy from the village walked toward the canal kicking a stone ahead of him. He gave a final kick that sent the stone high into the air. It fell into the water with a loud splash.

The boy looked up and saw the blue water. He waved his arms and shouted to the people. They came running and stood looking at the canal.

"Wampum Eater has answered our call," said their chief. "The woman of the fog has dug our canal."

So the Desert People had water for their crops of corn, pumpkins, squash and melons. And they prospered and lived in peace for many years. Often they thought of the old woman of the fog. On cold mornings when jagged peaks were hidden by the mists the people said, "Wampum Eater walks over the mountains today."

The Evil Spirits of Crooked Mountain

FOR the Desert People there were times of peace and times of war.

There was a long time of peace when they prospered and increased in numbers. But there was a time when the desert was a great battleground, when every mountain was a fortress, when an enemy might wait behind every rock.

The fiercest enemies of the Desert People were the Apaches—the Mountain Dwellers. Their deeds of bravery and endurance in battle were told around council fires across the valleys.

So skillful were the Apaches in concealing themselves that they could approach an enemy village in barren flat country without being seen. The attack was sudden. A sentinel fell, an arrow in his back. Out of the silent dawn, howling Apache warriors swarmed over the village. Soon only smoke and flames, rising as if from a huge funeral pyre, marked the place where the village had been.

The wars went on, sometimes in favor of the Desert People, sometimes in favor of the Mountain Dwellers. Many times the Desert People sent warriors into Apache country. Sometimes the warriors never returned. Other times they returned with many Apache scalps.

Some of the most bitter battles were fought between the Desert People living along the river south of Salt River Mountain and a group of Apaches living in a valley on the south side of Crooked Mountain. For many years the two peoples slashed away at each other. Sometimes they met in open battle, sometimes in forays of only a few braves on either side.

Early one morning in the quiet pre-dawn the riverside village was sleeping. A stirring like the soft west wind caused a few people to turn in their sleep. The whinnying of horses woke Chief Bounding Elk and many of his braves. In an instant they were at their doorways. They heard the muffled thunder of horses' hooves in the distance.

Chief Bounding Elk and his braves ran to the corrals where dust still hung in the air. One of the corrals was empty—and many of the best horses were gone.

The chief turned toward the east, toward Crooked Mountain. His lips were tight. Early morning light shone on a cloud of dust rising from the desert. When

Bounding Elk spoke his voice was a whisper, like the sound of flying arrows.

"The Mountain Dwellers of the South have done this," he said. "It is the Apaches of Crooked Mountain who have stolen our horses. We will circle around them." His hand made a great sweeping motion. "We can ride faster than they because we will not be driving a herd of horses. When they reach their home at Crooked Mountain they will find a surprise waiting for them."

95

Soon Bounding Elk and two hundred of his braves were riding over the desert toward the south end of Crooked Mountain. The sun rising over the mountain threw long shadows across the valley. The warriors could see the great cloud of dust far to the north. They knew they were riding faster than the Apaches.

They rode hard. Gradually the long shadows shortened. Foam from the mouths of the horses told them they had left the level desert and were on the long southern slope of the mountain. Up the long slope the horses labored, their heavy breathing accenting the sound of their hooves.

When the sun was almost overhead Bounding

Elk and his men rode into the cool shadows of the boulders. The chief led the way through winding passageways, over rocky ledges. Soon they were at an opening leading to a deep canyon, the narrow entrance almost hidden by overhanging palo verde limbs.

Bounding Elk brushed aside the limbs and rode into the narrow canyon. Great jagged cracks were clawed deep into the sides of the canyon. Here and there out of the steep walls shadowy rocks thrust their silhouettes against the sky. High above them the canyon rim glistened in the sunlight.

They rode slowly now. At last one by one they

filed through a red sandstone passageway at the far end of the canyon.

In the quiet of early afternoon Bounding Elk and his war party watched and waited. They were on the high ground beyond the canyon. From behind the web-like growth of a palo verde grove they looked out over a small green valley. Beneath them, near the center of the valley, the brown brush *wickiups* of the Apaches stood like giant bee hives.

Bounding Elk slowly raised his hand. Suddenly he brought it down with a shout. His knees pressed against his horse's withers. Snorting, the animal leaped forward. Down the rocky slope the warriors clambered, their shouts shattering the still air. One of the riders stopped, took quick aim and arched a flaming arrow into the wickiups.

Through the village the warriors rode, lashing at the brush houses with their torches. Women and children and old men ran about in confusion.

The work was quickly done. The brush wickiups crackled loudly. Dense clouds of brown smoke billowed above the valley.

Back up the rocky rise the Desert People rode, hurling their torches into the trees and grass as they went. It was a blackened trail of smoke and ashes they left behind when Bounding Elk led his men back into the narrow canyon. The men filed through the passageway more quickly this time. In their excitement they rode faster, without caution.

The last one had urged his horse into the canyon when suddenly the mountain shook with cries of terror. Three men fell from their horses. One lay face down. An arrow, still vibrating, protruded from his back.

Bounding Elk's keen eyes glanced over the canyon walls to the rocky rim above. He could see no one.

But at that moment one of the large boulders on the high rim toppled—slowly at first—then with bounding leaps came crashing down the steep wall. Large chunks of rock were plowed loose by the boulder. Many of the men had dismounted and were running toward the passageway through which they had just ridden. With a roar that shook the canyon the boulder and rubble poured into the midst of the fleeing men. Loud echoes answered each other through the canyon. Bounding Elk's horse reared and whinnied. Its eyes flashed white with sudden fear.

Some of the warriors were running toward the far end of the canyon. A hail of arrows stopped them.

Chief Bounding Elk drew an arrow and placed it

across his bow. He searched the ridges above for some movement. He could see none. An arrow, seemingly from nowhere, struck him. He fell to the ground and did not move.

When the men saw their chief lying motionless they threw their bows and arrows to the ground and crowded toward the canyon entrance. Above their cries they heard a rumbling noise high over their heads. Two of them had reached the passageway when with a crash that shook the ground another boulder fell into the midst of the fleeing men.

For a moment there was silence. Then the great rocks on the canyon walls began to topple as if pushed from behind. There was a low rumbling noise. The clawing cracks in the walls widened. Then, as if weary of the centuries, the walls loosened their hold on the mountain at last and fell crumbling to a common grave.

Only the two men returned to the village. When they told what had happened the people nodded their heads slowly. "It was the evil spirits of Crooked Mountain," they said.

But the Apaches tell another story. They say a few of their warriors, returning from raids along the Salt River, saw the smoke from their burning village.

They say their warriors knew they were too late to save their village and they also knew that the attackers would have to return through the narrow canyon. They say that these Apache warriors concealed themselves on the rim and killed Bounding Elk and his men below.

But the Desert People say that this cannot be. They say so many of their brave warriors could not have been defeated by a few Apaches, even in an ambush. They say their warriors were killed by the evil spirits of Crooked Mountain.

There are old ones among the Desert People who believe that if they went into this mountain today the evil spirits would shoot them with arrows from invisible bows, or send great rocks hurtling down upon them. And so, since the time long ago when their warriors were killed, many of the Desert People will not go into Crooked Mountain.

Children of Cloud

THERE was once a very beautiful woman who lived north of Crooked Mountain. She walked erect and held her head high. Her hair was as black as a raven's wing, and when the sun shone on it, it reflected the blue light of the sky.

Many brave and handsome men went to her parents and asked for their daughter in marriage. But each time she refused, and as the custom was among the Desert People, her refusal was final.

Often she showed her contempt for a suitor by waving a white eagle's feather, the symbol of the clouds, in front of him. In this way she told him,

"I would rather marry the clouds than marry you."

One day she was sitting on a high rock weaving mats of cane. She watched the rhythmic motion of her hands and after a time her eyelids became heavy. Soon she was asleep.

Now the cloud that hovered high over Crooked Mountain sent down a single drop of rain and it fell on the beautiful sleeping woman. Some time later she became the mother of twin boys.

Every man in the village claimed the twins for his own, for each one wanted to marry her. But the woman said, "No man shall be father to them, for their father is Cloud."

One day when the boys were about four years old their mother showed them the great white cloud banked high over Crooked Mountain. "That is your father," she said, pointing. "His name is Cloud. And Wind is your uncle, your father's older brother." The twins ran away and chased each other about and showed no interest.

But when they were about ten years old, they heard the other boys of the village speak of their fathers:

"My father can run faster than the fastest deer."

"My father is a brave warrior."

"My father has many Apache scalps."

"My father is a great hunter."

So the twins began to ask their mother about their father. Again she pointed to the cloud over the mountain. "He is still there," she said, "always watching over us."

The boys stood looking at the mountain and the cloud above. After a time one of them said, "My brother and I must go and see our father."

And their mother said, "You are young, but you are children of Cloud, and so you are brave. Go. Nothing shall harm you. Climb Crooked Mountain. Go and see your father. And do everything he tells you to do, for he is very wise." And she turned her head so that she would not see them as they walked away over the slopes of Crooked Mountain.

Soon they were at the foot of huge boulders. For a moment they stood looking up. Then, grasping a ledge, they began to climb. They moved swiftly.

Now Cloud saw them coming and watched them struggle up the steep mountain. At length they stood on the highest peak at the vast doorway to the house of Cloud. Cloud covered their eyes with fog so they could not see him. "Why have you come here?" he asked.

"We have come to see our father," they told him. "We are the children of Cloud."

Then Cloud took away the fog from their eyes.

"I am Cloud," he said, "but I wonder if it is true that you are really my children."

"So we have been told from the beginning," one boy said.

Cloud looked at them for a time without speaking. At last he said, "How can you prove that you are my children?"

The boys opened their mouths. Peals of thunder rolled out, and bolts of lightning flashed from their eyes.

"It must be true that you are my children," Cloud said. His smile was as broad as the mountain. And he fixed them a supper of corn and pumpkin.

When night came over the desert and mountains and darkened the sky, Cloud put the boys out of his house and shut the door. A cold rain began to fall. A little later a bitter north wind began to blow. Snow fell and clung to the icy ledges.

The cold wind lashed out at the boys but they felt no harm. "It is our uncle come to visit us," they said. "It is our uncle, the wind."

Early in the morning when Cloud came out of his house and saw that all was well with the twins, he said, "It must certainly be so. You must be my own children."

The next night Cloud took the twins to a pond where pieces of ice glistened on the water. He left the boys there and returned to his house. In the morning when Cloud moved over the crevices toward the pond he felt the icy wind against his face. But when he came to the pond he found the boys in the water, talking and laughing. Icicles hung from their clothing and ice crystals glistened in their black hair.

"Yes, it is absolutely true," Cloud said. "You are

indeed my own children. I will take you into my house."

For a time the boys lived happily with their father. When the people asked for rain the twins raced through the sky with Cloud, their father, and Wind, their uncle. They helped create the shafts of lightning and the peals of thunder that split the dark sky and told the people in the valley when the rain would fall.

But after a time the boys began to miss their vilage. "It would be good to see our mother again," said one.

"Let us speak to our father about it," said the other.

Cloud smiled down at them. "You may go back," he said. "But you must speak to no one on the way—no matter whom you meet. I will watch over you as you go."

So down the mountain went the boys with Cloud hovering over them to shield them from the hot sun. They reached the foot of the mountain and began to walk down the long slope when they saw a man from their village coming toward them.

"Let us ask him if all is well with our mother," said one brother.

"Remember Cloud, our father, is watching over us," said the other, "and he warned us not to speak to anyone."

"Yes, that is true," replied the first, "but it would not be right not to ask about our mother."

So when they drew close to the man the first brother called out, "How are our people in the village and how is it with our mother?"

Before the man could answer, Cloud surrounded them and made the desert dark as night. Lightning coursed through the sky and thunder split the air.

As suddenly as he had descended Cloud lifted. Where the boys had been standing now grew two tall green plants with long spiked leaves near the ground. From each cluster of leaves a slender green shaft reached upward toward the sky.

These plants are called century plants, for in olden times it was thought that they bloomed but once in a hundred years. They often grow side by side, and when they bloom their white cloud-like blossoms reach upward toward the sky.

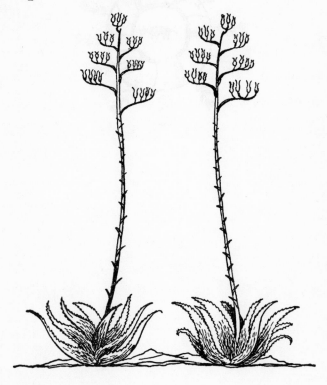